Jan Burchett and Sara Vogler were already friends when they discovered that they both wanted to write books for children – and that it was much more fun to write together. They meet every weekday for gossip, jokes and writing. If one is stuck for an idea, the other always comes up with something, or makes a cup of tea. They both have two children who are always their first audience.

Jan used to be a primary school teacher and lives in Essex. Sara used to be a midwife and lives in London.

All Little Terrors titles can be ordered at your local bookshop or
are available by post from Book Service by Post (tel: 01624 675137).

Little Terrors

Gruesome Twosome

Jan Burchett and Sara Vogler

Illustrated by Judy Brown

MACMILLAN
CHILDREN'S BOOKS

For Hilary Delamere and Sarah Maddock –
who are not at all gruesome!

First published 1999 by Macmillan Children's Books
a division of Macmillan Publishers Limited
25 Eccleston Place, London SW1W 9NF
Basingstoke and Oxford

Associated companies throughout the world

ISBN 0 330 37605 5

1 3 5 7 9 8 6 4 2

A CIP catalogue record for this book is available from the British Library.

Typeset by SX Composing DTP, Rayleigh, Essex
Printed and bound in Great Britain by Mackays of Chatham plc, Kent

Chapter One

George Brussell slammed the huge front door of Little Frightley Manor. He raced across the courtyard, pelted past the port-cullis and dashed over to the luxury caravan in the front garden where his friends lived.

When George moved into Little Fright-ley Manor, once the home of the noble Ghoulstone family, he'd been hoping that the grounds and gallery, battlements and basements, corridors and cubbyholes would be full to the brim with ghastly Ghoulstone ghouls. After all, over their seven hundred year history the family had met some very nasty and interesting deaths. But the only Ghoulstone ghosts who'd stayed at the rambling old house were seven feeble little spectres, who were too scared to be ghastly or ghoulish and lived in their caravan in the front garden.

George flung the caravan door open and poked his freckled nose inside.

"It's only me!" he called quickly, before his phantom friends could make their usual dive for cover.

"Master George!" huffed a wheezy voice. Edgar Jay, the ghost of an elderly, upright vacuum cleaner, trundled out wagging his nozzle disapprovingly. "Kindly knock before bursting in and frightening the spectral stuffing out of us!"

"*My* spectral stuffing is fine," declared a rather scruffy, singed spook. Florence Ghoulstone checked herself in the mirror and gave her scorched ringlets a casual tweak. "George didn't scare *me*."

"I saw you wobble, Flo!" scoffed her tatty twin brother. "You were so see-through you nearly disappeared altogether."

"I didn't!"

"You did!"

"I did not!" shouted Flo. "You must have soot in your eyes, Maggot!"

Flo and Maggot Ghoulstone had become ghosts all of a sudden when they'd blown

2

up the old west wing of Little Frightley Manor back in 1857, but it hadn't stopped them arguing. They'd been experimenting with the ingredients of the fuel for their father's latest invention, the horseless cart. Ever afterwards, they each insisted it had been their idea to add the deadly bananas – although it was Maggot who still smelt of barbecued fruit.

"Stop arguing, you two," laughed George. "Something's arrived for you all."

"Be it treasure?" demanded the ghost of a nine-year-old pirate. Mary Ghoulstone, scarred, bloodstained and weather-beaten, was always on the lookout for booty. She prowled eagerly around George.

"Pieces of eight?" squawked a one-eyed green parrot from Mary's shoulder. Duck had died a hero's death, walking the plank, blindfolded and with his wings tied behind his back.

"Not exactly," said George. "It's a letter."

The ghosts looked at each other in alarm.

"Who could it be from?" quavered Flo.

"No one knows we're here," whispered Maggot. "Do they?" He wiped his runny nose on his sooty sleeve. He'd had a cold on the day he died and he still had it – despite being blown up.

"When I cleaned for Lady Cecily," huffed Edgar Jay importantly, "she received correspondence daily – invitations to the theatre, letters from friends and offers of marriage. She always looked forward to opening her letters. Well, usually." Edgar Jay had suddenly remembered the dreadful morning in 1931 when Harrods had written to tell her ladyship that they had run out of her favourite toilet water.

"Maybe it's from one of your old relatives," said George eagerly.

The little ghosts paled at the thought of their awful ancestors.

"Hope not," whispered Flo.

A piece of ghostly paper fluttered out from a wardrobe. There was a list written on it. This was the work of Bartholomew Otherington-Smythe. Boss, as he was known, was so timid that he couldn't be seen or heard, and was too frightened to tell how he had died.

The Unknown Letter
by Bartholomew Otherington-Smythe

1. *I received only one letter in my thirteen years of life.*
2. *I was surprised and delighted.*
3. *As a poor relation of the Ghoulstones, most people ignored me.*
4. *So the joy of opening the envelope knew no bounds.*
5. *Until I discovered it was not for me at all.*
6. *And was intended for Barry the boot boy.*
7. *Therefore today is the first time I have received a letter.*
8. *I suggest we open it.*
9. *At once.*

"Wow!" gasped George. "What's happened to you, Boss? I thought you'd be cowering in the cupboard at the thought of something as scary as a letter!"

The piece of paper began to shake as a postscript appeared.

PS Bother! Now I have remembered to be scared.

"Belay there and stop all this jawing!" shouted Mary. She held out a grimy hand. "Give me the letter. I'll see what it's all about in the shake of a shark's tail."

"Good plan, Mary," laughed George, "with only two small drawbacks. I haven't got the letter with me – and you can't read."

Mary poked him angrily in the ribs with her cutlass. George squirmed. Spectral swords only tickle the living.

"Where is this letter then?" demanded Flo.

"It's in the house," said George. "On the mat by the front door. I can't pick it up – it's a spectral letter."

"That means we have to go inside Little Frightley Manor," quavered Maggot, wobbling at the edges.

Little Frightley Manor may not have

had any resident ghosts but it did have Sharren and Darren Brussell. George's parents wouldn't have seen a spook if it sawed itself in half and produced a rabbit out of a hat. In fact, George's large and lumbering father could walk through spectral stuffing without batting an eyelid, and George's mother could shriek the house down without any help from ghosts.

The anxious little ghosts stood close to George, staring at the ghostly letter that glowed on the doormat of Little Frightley Manor. Edgar Jay began to trundle nervously up and down the vast hall of his old cleaning patch.

"Where are your parents, Master George?" he huffed. The long-nosed pattern on his dust bag twitched anxiously.

"Mum's at the gym and Dad's having a working lunch in the conference room with some clients," explained George. "They won't be around for ages."

"Then we must open this letter im-

mediately," puffed the old hoover. "It could be a vital communication."

Nobody made a move to pick up the letter. There was a sudden, snuffling sound from Maggot's sooty shirt. The ghosts all jumped with fright. A small see-through snout appeared.

"Only me!" squeaked a little voice.

"It's Slightly!" gasped Maggot in relief. He reached into his sailor suit shirt and brought out something that looked like a crushed pincushion on legs. Slightly Flat-

Hedgehog had met his death at the local zoo under the rear end of Vera, the Vietnamese pot-bellied pig.

"Scared you all!" squeaked Slightly, delighted to see the pale faces of his friends.

"This is an auspicious occasion, young Slightly," puffed Edgar Jay. "We have a letter." He blew the envelope towards Flo, who picked it up gingerly.

"Open it then," said Maggot impatiently.

"You open it," said Flo, pushing it into his hand.

"No, you!"

"You!"

"Master Magnus! Miss Florence!" huffed the old hoover. "Please show some breeding. Even eight-year-old Ghoulstones should be capable of some sort of noble behaviour. One of you open the letter and read it to the rest of us."

Flo stuck out her lip sulkily and tore open the envelope. She unfolded the paper and began to read:

Spectral Company Regulating
Eerie Apparitions in Mansions

Dear resident ghosts,

It has come to the attention of SCREAM that Little Frightley Manor has not been visited for some time. Under our regulations, a prime site such as yours should house only hair-raising and horrifying haunters. Therefore a spectral inspector will call to make a spot check.

"What be an inspector?" demanded Mary. Pirates didn't have time for inspections. They were too busy stealing treasure and running people through with swords.

"An inspector makes sure that you're doing a good job," explained George.

The ghosts faded at the thought of doing a good job in the haunting department. That would mean bloodstains, wailing and staying up at night.

"And he's going to do a spot check!" whimpered Maggot. "None of us died of anything spotty."

A triumphant spectral note fluttered in the air.

I have spots!

"That's all very well, Boss," sighed George, "but the inspector might have trouble seeing them. Anyway, a spot check just means you could be inspected at any time, without warning."

The ghosts looked around the huge hall to see if any strange spooks were lurking. Except for Flo, who was staring aghast at the letter and wobbling violently at the knees.

"There's a PS!" she wailed. "*'Any ghost that fails the inspection must leave Little Frightley Manor – for ever!'*"

Chapter Two

"How can we be horrifying and hair-raising?" gasped Maggot. "No one ever shrieks at the sight of us. They never *see* us."

George looked at the singed twins, the pirate, the parrot with his eyepatch, the vacuum cleaner, the squashed hedgehog and the list. The only way they would ever make him shriek was with laughter.

"And we can't leave Little Frightley Manor," said Flo nervously. "It would be the end of us."

The little ghosts were tied to their old home by a sort of spectral gravity. If they went too far away they began to feel as if someone had pulled the plug out and their spectral stuffing was whooshing down the drain. If they were banned and could never come back, they would disappear for good.

"You won't have to leave!" declared George firmly. "You're going to practise

12

haunting. By the time this inspector calls, you'll be wailing, groaning and depositing bloodstains like the best of them. Come on."

He led the way into the huge lounge and plonked himself down on one of the luxurious sofas.

"Now I'll sit here minding my own business, and you try to scare me." The ghosts looked blankly at him. "Get on with it then. You're not frightening anyone standing there like lemons."

The feeble phantoms huddled together. Then they all disappeared behind the electronic grand piano. George waited. Nothing happened. Eventually, just as he was nodding off, six spooks leapt out onto the Persian rug at his feet and stood there, arms, wings and nozzle flapping wildly.

"What's next?" hissed Flo.

Mary turned to the piano and beckoned urgently with her cutlass. A small piece of paper appeared in front of George with *Boo!* written on it.

George burst out laughing. "That was hopeless!" he exclaimed. "I want to see

chains rattling, I want my flesh to crawl, I want cold, clammy hands, I want blood-curdling shrieks . . ."

"Shrieks?" huffed Edgar Jay anxiously. "Your mother isn't home, is she?"

". . . I want my hair to stand on end . . ."

"That'll be easy!" sniggered Flo, looking at George's spiky haircut.

". . . You've got to go through walls," continued George, getting well into his stride.

"But we get stuck!" wailed Maggot.

". . . You've got to float menacingly," insisted George.

Flo screwed up her face in concentration, closed her eyes and gave a little hop.

"Did I do it?" she asked.

"No, you didn't!" scoffed Maggot. "Don't know why you're bothering. Last time you tried to float you stepped off George's bed and fell on your face in his football boots."

"I did not!"

"Did!"

"Did not. I was demonstrating a diving tackle!"

Edgar Jay trundled off and began to blow at the wall. This was all the cleaning he could manage since the small electrical accident that had made him a ghost.

"What are you doing?" asked George. "You're supposed to be horrifying, not hoovering!"

"I apologize, Master George," huffed the old vacuum cleaner, embarrassed. "I was removing a stubborn speck of dust from the skirting board. However, I was doing it in a particularly menacing manner."

"*I'll* scare the breeches off you, George!"

declared Mary. "Duck and me will show you lot how to strike terror into lily-livered hearts. I weren't known as the Scourge of the Seven Seas for nothing." She leapt from couch to couch, slashing the air with her cutlass.

"Scourge of the Seven Sofas!" squawked Duck, fluttering off to attack the plastic moose head above the fireplace.

Mary shinned up the curtains and, growling like a mad dog, swung her way across the room from chandelier to chandelier. "Prepare to have your throats slit!" she cried. Suddenly she ran out of light fittings, swung into thin air and collided with the video collection on the opposite wall.

"Not quite what I had in mind," said George, giggling. "Funny – but not scary."

"Scared me!" squawked Duck, picking himself up from the fireplace.

"I'll have to show you," said George. "Follow me."

He tugged his tatty sweatshirt over his head like a hood, pulled a ghastly face, made claws of his hands and stomped round the room. "*Whooooooo!*" he howled. "*Eeeeeeee* . . . Come on, join in."

Looking more like a cautious caterpillar than a horde of avenging spirits, the ghosts trickled after George as he wove in and out of the furniture. "Louder!" shouted George, waving his arms madly. "That's more of a whinge than a wail. I want you to rattle the rafters and blast the—"

He stopped suddenly. The little ghosts shunted into each other with a series of spectral thuds. There, in front of George, was an apparition. It was the ghost of a small, thin man who shone with a dull, grey light. The figure wore a grey suit with a grey wing collar and a grey tie. He had a grey bowler hat on his head and thick, grey, pebble spectacles perched on his nose. He held a leather-bound book in one hand, a quill pen in the other, and he floated silently and solemnly above the carpet.

The chilling apparition opened his book and cleared his throat.

"Are you the ghosts of Little Frightley

Manor?" he asked. His voice was as cold and dead as he was.

The ghosts nodded faintly.

"I am Dilbert Dishwater, chief inspector of SCREAM. I have been watching you at work."

"That was only a practice," said George hurriedly. "Come back next week and I guarantee they'll frighten the socks off you."

"I'm afraid it's too late for that," said the spectral inspector coldly. "I have seen enough. These ghosts are the most feeble

examples of ectoplasm I have ever had the misfortune to come across." He carefully wrote his signature at the bottom of a piece of grey paper and held it out. Across the paper in big grey letters was one word.

Failed!

Chapter Three

"You must vacate the premises immediately," intoned the grey ghost.

"Hang on a minute," protested George. "You've hardly given them a chance. They only got your letter ten minutes ago!"

Mr Dishwater stared stonily at him. Ghosts have no concept of time passing. In fact, George's friends were lucky that the inspector hadn't turned up before Phantom Force had delivered the letter.

"Their family's been here for over seven hundred years," pleaded George. "Surely they're entitled to stay."

"They do not fulfil the requirements of SCREAM," droned Mr Dishwater.

"But look at these two," said George, pointing at Flo and Maggot. "They blew up the entire west wing of Little Frightley Manor. Surely that must count for something?"

"Not unless they can do it again."

The singed brother and sister looked at each other hopelessly. They had no idea how to blow themselves up. It had been an accident the first time.

A list appeared in front of Mr Dishwater's cold, grey eyes.

Reasons to be fearful
by Bartholomew Otherington-Smythe

1. *May I suggest that you should be scared of the Ghoulstone ghosts, Mr Dishwater?*
2. *Magnus and Florence squabble like harpies.*
3. *Edgar Jay can trundle in a terrifying manner.*
4. *Mary can say "Aha!" in a most alarming way.*
5. *And her parrot is a terrible enemy.*
6. *If you are allergic to feathers.*

Mr Dishwater pushed the list aside. The quivering paper folded itself up neatly and hid under a cushion.

Mary Ghoulstone drew her cutlass and stepped forward boldly. "You won't get rid of me!" she growled.

The ghosts gasped at her bravery. Mary looked terrifying, with her wild, dark hair, tattered and bloodstained clothes, and Captain Redbeard's dagger sticking out of her chest. Even Captain Redbeard had been scared of her. He'd only had the nerve to stab her when she was looking the other way. Duck perched fiercely on her shoulder, fixing Mr Dishwater with his one beady eye. Perhaps the pirate and her parrot could save them!

At that moment the door to the west wing opened, and in walked Darren Brussell. "Hello there, George," he said when he saw his son, standing on his own in the middle of the room. "This way, gents," he called over his shoulder. A line of businessmen in dark suits filed into the lounge on their way from a business lunch in Darren's conference room.

"Go on, Mary!" whispered Flo, taking refuge behind George.

"Fifteen men all dressed in their best," squawked Duck, hiding in Mary's hair. "Yo ho ho and lunch in their tums!"

Surely Mr Dishwater would have to let them stay if Mary could scare all these men in suits.

The bold buccaneer leapt forward with an almost ghostly howl. She planted herself defiantly in front of the advancing line, cutlass swishing and eyebrows bristling.

Darren and his colleagues marched straight through her and filed out into the hall. Mary stood there rocking in their wake.

Mr Dishwater shook his head pitilessly and pointed to the door.

"Perhaps my friends could stay in my bedroom?" suggested George.

"Or we could promise to go back to our caravan and never budge," begged Flo.

The grey ghoul stared at her blankly.

"We could go and live by the lake, or down at the gate?" huffed Edgar Jay desperately. "We could bivouac in the bushes."

"You are to leave immediately," said Mr Dishwater coldly, "or it will be the worse for you." He turned to George and opened

23

his book. "How many living people are there here?"

"Don't think you're going to get me and my parents to leave," said George firmly, "or the housekeeper and her husband."

"Five," said Mr Dishwater, writing in his book. "Enough to be going on with."

And with that he turned and floated through the wall.

There was a scuffling noise near the fireplace and something moved in the magazine rack. Slightly Flat-Hedgehog rolled out and unscrolled himself. "I was stuck," he squeaked. "Spines got caught. Where's that inspector?" The little hedgehog stood with his flattened spines quivering fiercely. "I'll scare him!"

"It's too late for that, Slightly," quavered Maggot. "He's turned us out."

"You won't have to go," said George firmly. He strode up and down, deep in thought. "Anyway, what can he do to you, a weedy little grey man like him? It's not as if he's going to whack you with his book or stab you with his pen nib. He couldn't

hurt a fly, let alone a phantom. Come on, we'll . . ."

But his little friends had gone. Both the doors of the lounge were open so George knew they could be anywhere. He had to find them quickly. They were such a bunch of scaredy spooks that they might be making plans to run away at that very minute!

There was no sign of any small spectres heading for the gates so they had to be somewhere in the house. George went into the west wing and past the door to his father's office. He was about to bound up the spiral staircase that led to his bedroom, when he heard a familiar, dull voice coming from his father's conference room at the end of the corridor. He pushed open the door.

Darren's conference room took up the whole ground floor of the Victorian tower. A long table, covered in the remains of a business lunch, stood in the centre, and around the walls were computer screens, overhead projectors and flip charts. In pride of place was a huge oil painting of Sharren Brussell dressed as a shepherdess.

In between the coffee machine and the photocopier, sat Mr Dishwater. His book and quill were neatly laid out in front of him on a grey spectral desk and behind him hung a small, pale photograph of a grey woman in a grey dress. The inspector from SCREAM was talking into an old-fashioned telephone. He had clearly set up an office at Little Frightley Manor.

"...Yes, sir...Absolutely, sir...Everything is ready for tonight, sir."

He hooked the mouthpiece on to the stand and gave George a blank stare.

"I was hoping you'd gone," said George.

"Hoping I'd gone, George?" said Darren, bursting into the room. "After my computer games, were you?"

"Why couldn't you let them stay?" George pleaded with Mr Dishwater.

"There was no need," said Darren, scratching his bald patch. "I'd given them lunch and they'd signed the contracts." He sat down at the big table and stuffed a vol-au-vent into his mouth.

"A house like this requires high-class haunters," said Mr Dishwater, looking at Darren distastefully. "And I have some rather special clients lined up."

Something caught George's eye and he peered out of the window.

"Looks like they're lined up already."

Mr Dishwater floated over to stare out in amazement across the courtyard where, winding its way around the portcullis, was a long, glowing queue of spooks.

Chapter Four

"You're right, George," said Darren.

George looked in surprise at his father. His dad had never seen a spook before! But Darren was looking down the drive to where his visitors' cars were lined up, waiting to turn out of the gates.

"Must be heavy traffic on the road," said Darren as he lumbered over to a computer.

Mr Dishwater was mesmerized by the sight of all the spooks in the courtyard.

"I don't understand!" he said. A flicker of panic passed over his dull, grey face. "There must be some mistake. What can they want?"

"Only one way to find out," said George. "Let's ask them."

"You can go and do a traffic survey if you want," said Darren, clicking on an icon. "I've got . . . work to do." He started playing Zap the Zargoids.

George rushed out of the door, along the corridor, through the lounge and the hall, and out of the front door. He found Mr Dishwater emerging through the wall of the conference room into the courtyard.

George was delighted to see so many spooks but Mr Dishwater floated back and forth, flapping his book. George went straight up to the head of the queue where a harmless-looking ghost hovered, wearing a tweed cloth cap on his head and clutching an old vacuum flask.

"What's going on?" asked George.

The spectre pulled a copy of the *Weekly Wailer* out from his pocket.

"We've heard that Little Frightley Manor is up for grabs. I've come to move in."

"So have I!" chanted the ghost of a monk who was second in the line.

"And me!" called the head of a Cavalier from under its arm.

Mr Dishwater floated over. George could have sworn there were one or two beads of grey sweat on his brow.

"Let me see that!" the inspector demanded. "There must have been a mistake."

"Certainly," said the man with the flask. He pointed to an item on the gossip page of the spectral newspaper.

"'*Little Frightley Manor*,'" read Mr Dishwater in an anxious voice, "'*the ancient home of the Ghoulstone family and scene of many a bloodthirsty death, has no gruesome ghouls!*' It's a misprint! When I contacted the newspaper, I told them to write *new* gruesome ghouls." He turned to the long queue in front of him and cleared his throat nervously. "This house is not available."

"Wait a minute," said George, horrified. "You'd planned the whole thing before you even got here! Even if my friends had been the scariest spooks since Sliced Fred, they were never going to pass your test." George had just finished a book about the ghost of a demon baker who made sandwiches with most unpleasant fillings.

"That is immaterial," said Mr Dishwater, waving his book in agitation. "My clients will be arriving shortly so you can all go and haunt somewhere else – and please take your body parts with you."

There were angry mutterings along the line.

"Oh woe is me!" wailed a white lady, wringing her hands and wafting up and down the queue, her voluminous skirts billowing out behind her. "I'm not budging!"

"It's taken me long enough to get myself together," complained a ghoul who had

31

suffered the Death of a Thousand Cuts and seemed to have a spare arm she didn't know what to do with. "So I'm staying put!"

"Who do you think you are anyway?" demanded the monk. "Telling us to go. It's not your house."

"That's right," said George fiercely. "This house belongs to the Ghoulstone ghosts."

"Not any more!" said Mr Dishwater coldly. "I represent the new spectral owners. And they will be very angry . . ."

A phantom with a bobble hat and a rattle wafted up to the head of the queue.

"If you don't hurry up, mate," he said crossly, "we're going to miss the kick-off."

"There is no football here," snapped Mr Dishwater.

"You want the recreation ground," said an old lady with a shopping bag and a gas mask. "Down the road and on your right."

The football fan turned and waved down the line.

"Wrong place, lads!" he called and set

off down the drive followed by half the queue.

"Get a move on up there," shrieked a banshee from the end of the line.

"I'm going in!" said the man with the vacuum flask.

"And me!" chanted the monk.

"And I," wailed the white lady.

"So am I," said the lady with the shopping bag, waving her gas mask. "You just try and stop me!"

George watched gobsmacked as almost every kind of ghost he could have imagined pushed past the protesting Mr Dishwater and through the closed front door of Little Frightley Manor.

Suddenly George remembered his little friends. He *had* to find them before they set eyes on all the new, uninvited guests. Their spectral stuffing would probably go all floppy with fear at the sight of a spectral vacuum flask, let alone a hooded monk or a wailing banshee.

Chapter Five

George ran into the hall past a ghost who was painstakingly painting spectral blood-stains on the flagstones, and the old lady with the gas mask who was patiently waiting outside the toilet under the stairs. He looked around the lounge, where a howling apparition was checking out the chimney breast and a man with an axe in his back was saying boo to the moose head over the fireplace. He peered into his dad's office. There was a choir of ghouls wailing at the windows. And in the dining room the white lady was walking up and down past the hostess trolley, wringing her hands.

Back in the hall, George dashed up the stone staircase, overtaking a moaning figure who was dragging his chains. There was an argument in one of the guest bedrooms. Two women in headscarves, who'd died when their bingo hall had

34

collapsed, were trying to outshriek each other. George couldn't imagine where his friends were hiding. Every room seemed to be seething with spooks who were trying to prove how scary they were. Little Frightley Manor had been invaded.

George's little friends were gibbering under the four-poster bed in his bedroom. They were too scared to leave Little Frightley Manor and were quaking with terror at the thought of what would happen if Mr Dishwater found them.

"What are we going to do?" whispered Flo. "We can't stay here for ever."

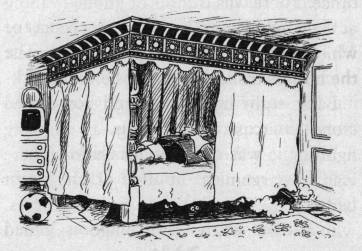

"And we can't scare anyone," wailed Maggot.

A trembling scrap of paper appeared.

Except ourselves.

"I can!" squeaked Slightly, snuffling fiercely at George's slippers.

At that moment someone came through the door – without opening it.

"It be Mr Dishwater!" whispered Mary. "He's come to make us walk the plank!"

"Not again!" squawked Duck, from under his wing. He didn't like to be re-minded of his death.

"I do not believe that those are the feet of Mr Dishwater," huffed Edgar Jay. The elderly hoover had spent most of his work-ing life studying carpets and considered himself an expert in footwear.

"Who is it then?" whimpered Maggot.

"I have no idea!" puffed Edgar Jay in terror.

A pair of shiny, ghostly boots glided

around the room. Then they disappeared as their occupant got up on the bed. After a while the bedroom was filled with the sound of spectral snoring.

"Let's get out of here," whispered Flo.

The little ghosts slithered out from under the bed. They could just see the boots and fancy clothes of the sleeping spectre. To their relief, the rest was hidden by the curtains of the four-poster bed.

They turned towards the door and froze in terror. There, on top of George's computer, dripping phantom blood down the screen, was the severed head of a ghostly Cavalier. The rest of him must be asleep on the bed! The snoring stopped and one eye slowly opened. With a whoosh, the little spooks made it through the closed bedroom door. Only in moments of extreme terror could they get through anything solid on the first attempt.

"There you are!" said a voice.

It was George. The feeble phantoms clung to him – as much as any ghost can cling to the living.

"Master George!" huffed Edgar Jay, trying to wrap his nozzle round George's leg. "There is a headless horror in your bedroom!"

"Only one?" said George. "You should see what we've got in the rest of the house."

The little ghosts virtually disappeared with shock.

"Have we been boarded?" whispered Mary.

"Shiver me feathers!" squawked Duck in alarm.

"Someone has spread a rumour that Little

Frightley Manor is crying out for creepy ghosts," said George, frowning. "And now the place is seething with spooks."

"What are we going to do?" wailed Maggot.

"Spike 'em!" squeaked Slightly ferociously from Maggot's shirt.

"Can't you get rid of them, George?" pleaded Flo.

Suddenly the whole house reverberated with the echoing sound of a bell. Spectres poured out from every nook and cranny and floated towards the stairs. The ghoul with the chains had just reached the top step and had to turn laboriously round to go all the way back down again.

"That ship's bell be calling me," growled Mary. She began to walk along the gallery as if pulled by a magnet.

"Don't go, Mary!" shouted Flo.

But suddenly all the little ghosts found their feet, wings and wheels propelled towards the stone staircase and the call of the bell.

"Might as well go and see what all the

39

fuss is about," said George, following them.

At the door of Darren's conference room was the ghost of a town crier, ringing his bell for all he was worth. Mr Dishwater had tried to call everyone together but none of the spectral inhabitants had taken any notice. The town crier, hearing the pathetic tones of the weedy grey spectre, had taken the opportunity to show off his skills.

Seventy-three assorted spooks were floating around the enormous room. It was lucky Darren had given up zapping the Zargoids and had gone to his study next door to do a bit of proper work. Even he would have noticed his papers flapping in the spectral breeze.

In spite of their terror, the little ghosts found themselves drawn into the room. Before Mr Dishwater could catch sight of them, they fled for the safety of the filing cabinet. All except Edgar Jay, who tried in vain to get into the bottom drawer and had to be content with gibbering behind a flip chart.

Mr Dishwater cleared his throat. The ghosts stopped to look at him. He rose in the air so that he could be seen by everyone, even the contortionist in the back row who had died when she sneezed in the middle of a trick.

"This will not do at all," announced the dull, grey ghoul. "A prime haunting site such as Little Frightley Manor deserves grade one ghosts and I have the very spooks lined up."

"Who are you to decide that?" asked an armoured spectre who was wearing a crown and had an arrow in his eye.

"I am the chief inspector of SCREAM," said Mr Dishwater coldly.

"Never heard of it," shouted a wraith.

"Do you have some identification?" asked a rather battered policeman who had unfortunately been on the scene when the first ever traffic light exploded.

"I do not need identification," said Mr Dishwater dismissively. "As I was saying, I have this place lined up for two rather special clients and I think you would all be interested to know who they are."

"Pray tell," chanted the monk.

"Arriving at nightfall and expecting to find the house phantom-free, are Mr Weird and Mr Feared."

There was a ripple of shock around the room.

"Weird and Feared!"

"That diabolical duo!"

"I've heard what they do to innocent victims!"

"I'm off!"

"Wait for me!"

There was a mass exodus of ectoplasm through the walls. The old lady with the gas mask hurried to catch up.

"'Ere!" she yelled. "Don't jump the queue."

This Weird and Feared must be a sight to see, thought George.

"I thought that would do the trick," said Mr Dishwater, rubbing his pale grey hands with satisfaction.

"Not quite," said George, pointing at a small group of ghouls in the corner.

"Weird and Feared?" said the man with

the flask. "I've heard of them. I bet I'm as scary as they are!"

"Oh lack-a-day!" wailed the white lady. "I'm not going back to my damp old tower. It plays havoc with my draperies." She arranged the folds of her nightgown and then went back to her hand-wringing.

"I'm not leaving either," said the ghost with the chains, plonking himself down on a chair. "It's taken me long enough to get here with this lot weighing me down!"

"I don't think you quite understand," said Mr Dishwater stonily. "Mr Weird and Mr Feared are—"

"There's only one way to sort this out," interrupted George suddenly. He was grinning. "You want Little Frightley Manor to be occupied by the very best in haunting. So let's have a Supreme Scaring Competition tonight. Every ghost can enter . . ."

"We can't!" came a frightened whisper from the top drawer.

George ignored it.

". . . and the spook – or spooks – who win get to stay and the others have to go."

43

"I think it's a grand idea," said the phantom with the vacuum flask.

"Let's do it!" said the ghost with the chains.

"There will be no competition," stated Mr Dishwater quickly. He was beginning to sound anxious. "My clients will ..." He glanced nervously at the looming group of determined-looking ghouls and a flicker of cunning passed over his expressionless grey face. "On second thoughts, my clients will be delighted." He peered at George through his thick glasses. "May I suggest that you, young man, as an example of the living, act as judge."

"Oh woe, alas!" wailed the white lady. "Better start practising."

George watched as the three competitors disappeared hastily to prepare for the evening. "May the best ghost win," he said, grinning.

Mr Dishwater pulled out a roll of spectral red carpet from a drawer in his ghostly desk and wafted over to the door. He had a cold, grey gleam in his eye as he turned to George.

"Oh, they'll win all right – just you wait and see!" he said.

Chapter six

"I thought you were trying to help us, George!" said Flo, sitting down in a huff on George's four-poster bed. "First of all we're ordered out by that Mr Dishwater . . ."

". . . and then you give him ideas for choosing our replacements!" added Maggot, flicking miserably through one of the football annuals that were scattered over George's bedroom floor.

"Hang on a minute . . . !" protested George.

"It be a stab in the back for this crew!" growled Mary disapprovingly. She had forgotten for a moment that any pirate worth his salt would cheerfully slaughter a fellow buccaneer whenever necessary.

"Abandon shipmates!" squawked Duck pitifully, from the window sill.

"Listen!" said George.

"What are we going to do?" wailed

Maggot. "It's getting dark and we're supposed to be long gone and that Weird and Feared will be coming and the contest will start and George will make new friends and forget all about us and—"

"You've got it all wrong," insisted George.

An agitated piece of ghostly paper appeared.

Our Dilemma
by Bartholomew Otherington-Smythe

1. *As George appears to have washed his hands of us, we have two choices.*
2. *We stay for the Supreme Scaring Competition.*
3. *And be scared away.*
4. *Or we leave Little Frightley Manor now as ordered by Mr Dishwater.*
5. *And fade away.*
6. *Oh calamity!*

"Now listen to me, you daft spooks!" shouted George. "Can't you see I'm trying to help you? I've got it all worked out.

Don't forget, the ghosts have to scare *me*."

"That will be difficult, Master George," huffed Edgar Jay, "if not impossible." George was rarely frightened by the super-natural – even when everyone else was telling him to run.

"Exactly!" said George cheerfully. "No one will win the competition, especially if Mum and Dad are there as well. So all the ghosts will have to leave and you'll have the place to yourselves again."

"Spooktacular!" exclaimed Flo.

"George be a shipmate loyal and true," declared Mary.

"I knew you were on our side, George," said Maggot smugly.

"No you didn't!" said Flo.

"Yes I did!" shouted Maggot.

"You didn't!" yelled Flo. "You said you would never speak to him again."

Suddenly Duck flew up from the window sill. "Vessel approaching below!" he squawked in alarm.

George ran to the bedroom window, followed timidly by the quivering ghosts.

48

They could see Mr Dishwater glowing by the front door below, his carpet tucked under his arm. He was looking down the drive.

And then, to their horror, they saw what he was looking at. A ghostly funeral carriage, pulled by four black spectral horses with black plumes on their heads, was slowly coming to a halt in front of Little Frightley Manor.

Mr Dishwater flung down the red carpet. It unrolled itself from the closed front door of the house, across the courtyard and over to the carriage steps. It lay there like a river of blood.

Mr Dishwater floated nervously along the carpet, opened the carriage door and cringed back like a frightened dog. Out swept a towering apparition swathed in a long black fur coat and carrying a cane. Its face was hidden from George and the ghosts by its black top hat and high collar. An identical figure followed. The two sinister spectres hovered side by side, surveying the front of Little Frightley Manor. Then, linking arms and knocking

49

Mr Dishwater aside, they floated along the red carpet and disappeared through the huge front door.

The little ghosts at the window stood silent and still, as if transfixed. George went over to the bedroom door.

"Looks like Weird and Feared have turned up," he said enthusiastically. "Don't seem very scary to me. Let's go down and have a look."

George marched along the landing towards the gallery that overlooked the huge stone

hall of Little Frightley Manor. His phantom friends trailed reluctantly behind him. With all these ghastly ghosts popping up everywhere they weren't going to let George out of their sight.

When George got to the banisters he stopped. The little ghosts cowered back in the shadows.

The two tall dark figures, still swathed in hats and long coats, were floating round the brightly lit hall below, examining the suit of armour, the ornate fireplace and the electronic grandfather clock. George peered down. The ghosts had their backs to him. To his surprise, George was relieved that he couldn't see their faces.

"Not bad, Dishwater," boomed one of the apparitions. His voice was like a hollow echo in an empty vault. "But the lighting is wrong."

Mr Dishwater rushed over to the dimmer switch. The glitter of the chandeliers faded. "That's better. Feels like home already. Much grander than our poky little theatre."

"I aim to please, Mr Weird, sir,"

simpered the weedy grey ghost, cringing in front of him.

"How many of the living are there?" snapped the other figure. The words cut the air like the edge of a butcher's knife.

"Five, Mr Feared, sir."

"*Five!*" boomed Mr Weird. "Couldn't you do better than that?"

"Five at present, I mean," whimpered the terrified grey ghost. "Now there is one small—"

"Did you have any trouble with the resident spooks?" demanded Mr Feared, tapping Dilbert smartly on the back with his cane.

"Oh no, Mr Feared," stammered Mr Dishwater, rubbing his shoulder. "They are long gone. A feeble bunch. I didn't tell them I was your agent. I pretended I was an inspector from SCREAM."

This produced a chuckle of cold laughter from Mr Weird and Mr Feared.

George was incensed. Mr Dishwater was nothing but an impostor inventing a false phantom organization.

"However," continued Mr Dishwater weakly, "there are . . ."

"There are *what*, Dishwater?"

"Out with it, you foolish ghoul!"

Dilbert Dishwater looked greyer than ever. He swallowed hard and nervously twisted his hands as he answered. "There are one or two other . . . erm . . . apparitions who have turned up, demanding to be allowed to haunt here. I couldn't get rid of . . . Oh dear! . . . I mean, I agreed they could stay. I . . . pretended there would be a scaring competition to choose the new resident . . . just so you could have the pleasure of driving them out yourselves, of course."

"You stupid spectre!" roared Mr Weird, swishing at the agent with his cane. "I'll pulverize your spectral stuffing!"

His voice echoed round the hall. George could hear the gibbering of the little spooks behind him and he felt an unexpected shiver go down his spine.

Dilbert Dishwater was cowering behind the suit of armour.

"Hold hard, Weird," said Mr Feared, grasping his partner's arm with a gloved hand. "Scaring competition, eh? Whom shall we scare?"

"If I might make so bold," spluttered Mr Dishwater, creeping out gingerly, "there is a living boy here who's seen all the other ghosts and not batted an eyelid. I think he'll change his mind when he sets eyes on you two gentlemen."

"Could be a bit of a lark, Weird," mused Mr Feared.

"We could have some audience participation, Feared!"

"Start our haunting of Little Frightley with a winning performance, Weird."

"Back on the stage at last, Feared."

"Top of the bill, Weird!"

And with a swish of their heavy coats, the two figures floated majestically through the closed door that led to the lounge.

Magicians Wally Weird and Fred Feared had been a double act on the Victorian music hall stage. It was difficult to tell them apart. They'd both been large, blubbery men, who were more like thugs than magicians. They weren't particularly good at their tricks, usually got booed off the stage and always blamed their failures on their downtrodden agent, Dilbert Dishwater.

Then, one night, it all changed. Mr Dishwater was in charge of their stage props and in his nervous agitation he failed to notice that he had ordered a box of real swords instead of retractable, false ones. This was unfortunate for the volunteer who climbed happily into the magic box that night for the grand finale. However, the audience went wild with excitement at the lifelike screams as Weird and Feared plunged the swords through the holes in the box and out the other side, dripping with particularly realistic blood.

Mr Dishwater watched in trepidation from the wings as the final curtain came down to rapturous applause. He was just wondering if he had time to run when he felt a heavy hand on his shoulder.

"Dishwater!" boomed Wally Weird.

"I apologize, Mr Weird, sir," squeaked Dilbert. "It won't happen again, I assure you."

"But we very much hope it will!" said Fred Feared, giving Mr Dishwater a sharp nudge in the ribs and closing one eye in a long, horrible wink.

Dilbert Dishwater looked at them both blankly through his thick pebble glasses. Then the terrible truth dawned. "Certainly, Mr Feared, sir."

From then on, Weird and Feared's fame

soared, thanks to the sharp saw that Mr Dishwater bought from the ironmonger's instead of the joke shop, the razor-sharp knives for the knife throwing act, and the extra-strong gunpowder if anyone needed to be dispatched in a puff of smoke.

When Weird and Feared made somebody disappear . . . they disappeared. And for a long time no one in the audience noticed that they might have mislaid a relative or two after the excitement of seeing the famed duo at work. Weird and Feared became rich and ever more ambitious.

Then, one night in 1893, Wally Weird and Fred Feared themselves disappeared in the middle of an act and were never seen alive again.

Chapter seven

A phantom poster hung on the door of the lounge of Little Frightley Manor.

George sat on the sofa eating popcorn and waiting for the competition to begin. He could hear the ghost in chains and the white lady squabbling in the corridor about who was going first. He looked over the back of the sofa where his ghostly friends were gibbering in a bunch.

TONIGHT
SUPREME SCARING COMPETITION
STAR PRIZE
LITTLE FRIGHTLEY MANOR.
TOP OF THE BILL
THE GRUESOME TWOSOME
WEIRD & FEARED
(WITH SUPPORTING CAST)

"You lot all right down there?" he asked.

"Just tell us when it's over," whispered Flo, who had her hands over her eyes.

"Aye," hissed Mary, "give us a shout when the coast be clear. Not that I be scared!"

"Shaking like a jellyfish!" squawked Duck from under his wing.

At that moment Mr Dishwater floated in, turned down the lights and hovered, glowing greyly in the middle of the lounge. He was carrying a long, grey spectral stick with a large hook on the end like a shepherd's crook. "The Supreme Scaring Competition is about to start," he announced. "I will remind you of the rules. The winner is the one who can strike the most terror into this living boy here. First on the bill is Ghost in Chains."

The first competitor struggled out from the corridor, dragging his chains behind him. He began the long, slow trek across the carpet.

"While we're waiting," said Mr Dishwater impatiently, "competitor number two – Winifred Weeping, the white lady."

The white lady whooshed through the closed door, passed the trudging ghost in chains and gave a piteous wail. She was about to launch into her famous and terrifying hand wringing routine, when her fluttering skirts caught on Mr Dishwater's hook. The white lady and the grey ghoul fell to the floor in a tangle of phantom fabric.

"Very dramatic," said George, "but not what I'd call frightening."

Winifred Weeping got up in a fluster, angrily arranged her skirts and opened her mouth, ready for a good, long howl.

"Thank you, number two," intoned Dilbert Dishwater, staggering to his feet and pulling her off by the neck with his stick.

The ghost in chains had just dragged himself past the first armchair.

"We seem to have time for Mr Stanley Hollowlegs," droned the grey ghost. "Apparently he has a little poem for us."

The ghost with the vacuum flask materialized in the middle of the carpet, took off his cap and bowed.

"You're the most harmless looking of the lot!" laughed George.

"We'll see, young sir," beamed Stanley. He struck a dramatic pose, his flask held high, and began:

There's a nice little factory in Creeply,
Where they make a good vacuum flask.
So when a leak sprang in my Thermos,
I had to go up there and ask,

"Can you help keep the heat in my bottle?"
The lad at reception seemed keen.
He said, "Go on through but be careful –
and mind the air-sucking machine!"

Now I were a bit hard of hearing,
And —

"Excuse me," broke in George, "but this isn't very scary." Mr Hollowlegs' monologue looked as if it was going to take all night.

"I hadn't got to the frightening bit," said the ghost, offended at the interruption. "There's twenty-five more verses to come yet."

Mr Dishwater waved his stick threateningly.

"All right," said Stanley Hollowlegs. "I'll go on to my demonstration of what the air-sucking machine did when it attached itself to my head."

And with that he removed his cloth cap, puffed out his cheeks and, with a ghastly slurping noise, turned completely inside out. He stood there, mangled, see-through and glowing blood-red. His spectral heart could be seen pumping away, sending ghostly blood round his arteries. His liver hung below his stomach, purple and juicy, and his intestines worked away, for ever digesting his last meal. His eyes dangled from their sockets and his brain glistened and pulsed gently. It was a disgusting sight.

"Wow!" gasped George.

Mr Dishwater started.

"Not scared, are you?" he asked anxiously.

"No," said George. "I think he looks great!"

George always enjoyed anything that involved gore and internal organs.

Stanley Hollowlegs sadly sucked in his blood- and muscle-covered cheeks and, with a slurp, slowly returned to normal.

"I must be losing my touch," he said, puzzled, as Mr Dishwater pulled him off.

The ghost in chains had finally made it to the middle of the carpet. He was so exhausted by his long trek that he collapsed on a sofa and closed his eyes. The grey ghoul prodded him with his stick, but competitor number one didn't move.

Mr Dishwater floated over to hover in front of George. For once his eyes shone with an excited glow. "And now prepare to be petrified. Get ready to be riveted with fear. Hold on to your seat in anticipation of the horrors to come. Straight from their haunt at the Hauntingdon Hippodrome, I proudly present . . . the Gruesome

Twosome!" He flung out his arm towards the door that led to the west wing.

To everyone's surprise, the door to the hall suddenly opened and into the darkened room came two figures. One glowed with a luminous, deep red glow and the other scratched its bald patch and looked over at George.

"What are you doing on your own in the dark, son?" he asked.

The ghastly crimson figure turned up the lights. Mr Dishwater recoiled at the sight of Sharren in her fluorescent, hooded housecoat and with her huge, blond hairdo swathed in a matching scarf. Darren lumbered over to his drinks bar. George wished Mr Dishwater would use his hooked stick on these two.

"As I was saying," began Mr Dishwater irritably. "I proudly present—"

"Cocktail, Shazza?" asked Darren. "What spirit do you want in it?"

"I fancy some gin!" shrieked Sharren, sitting next to George and opening a pot of scarlet nail varnish.

"I'll fix you a White Lady then," said Darren, consulting a chart.

"Did somebody call?" wailed the white lady hopefully, thinking that perhaps she'd won the competition.

Mr Dishwater hovered over the carpet. "Pay attention!" he snapped. "And now, by popular demand, I present . . . the great Weird and Feared!"

The lights went down once again and two spectral spotlights picked out the door to the west wing.

"What's wrong with the lights?" shrieked Sharren.

"Leave them, Shazza," said Darren, throwing slices of lemon and cucumber into a long glass. "Adds to the atmosphere."

George looked over to the spectral rings of light. Two huge apparitions in their long dark coats and top hats were gliding effortlessly through the closed door. They were hiding their faces deep in their fur collars.

"Prepare to be terrified!" boomed the first.

"After you, Weird."

"No, after you, Feared!"

"Together then?"

The two spooks threw off their coats with a flourish. Two ghastly white spectral skeletons, with gaping eye sockets, loomed over George. Their mouths were fixed in a grim grin and their bones rattled and clashed together.

George shrank back in horror against the cushions.

Chapter Eight

Wally Weird and Fred Feared had not intended to disappear for ever that night back in 1893. It had been a bit of a mistake. The Gruesome Twosome had been visited that day by a police detective, who was making enquiries about the disappearance of every member of their audiences who had ever taken part in any of their tricks. Weird and Feared invited the detective to come to the theatre that night and watch them plunge into a tank seething with piranha fish. They would emerge intact and prove that there was absolutely no skulduggery involved in their tricks, just skilful magic. The detective agreed, little knowing that Weird and Feared were sizing him up for their grand finale – the human cannon ball.

They sent Dishwater off to buy a huge fish tank, some weed and the fish.

"Remember, Dishwater," boomed Mr Weird with a wink, "the last thing we want is *real* piranhas!"

Mr Dishwater had not heard the cunning plan and dutifully wrote *real piranhas* as the last thing on his list. After all, he was used to doing exactly what his employers told him to, without question.

No one was more surprised than Weird and Feared when they leapt into the tank of what they thought were harmless goldfish. It only took the piranhas a few seconds to pick their bones clean.

George didn't normally mind the sight of a spectral bone or two. But there was something absolutely horrifying about the two leering skeletons that stood in front of him in their top hats, shirt-fronts and ragged cuffs. A ghostly piranha still clung by the teeth to the remains of Mr Weird's shirt. The sight of them made George think of empty tombs, echoing vaults, and bones piled high in the charnel house.

But it wasn't just their grotesque appearance that struck terror into George. Since their death, Weird and Feared had spent their time tormenting their spectral victims from the Hauntingdon Hippodrome, delighting in every despicable trick. They had grown ever more nasty and evil. However, after years of practising their diabolical trade on the same unfortunate ghosts, there wasn't much left to throw spectral knives at, or saw in half or explode. So they had sent their agent out in search of a suitably grand house, and living people – blood was much more interesting than spectral stuffing. And as soon as they set eyes on

George they knew they had found their first victim.

Now they towered over George, their grasping finger bones outstretched. He felt a deathly cold creep over him.

Mr Dishwater watched with grim satisfaction. Scaring this boy and winning the competition would be sure to put his masters in a good mood. They might even scare George to death. And he knew that they were very, very good at it – after all, they had done it to him. He would never forget his desperate escape from the theatre that fateful night after the piranha trick had gone wrong, and his utter terror when his two dead masters suddenly appeared in front of him. He would never forget the rattle of bones clamouring in his head. He would never forget his heart seizing up and his blood turning to ice in his veins.

Stanley Hollowlegs and the white lady cowered in the corner, the ghost in chains tried to hide under a cushion, and, from behind the sofa, George could hear terrified whimpers.

"Whatever's the matter, Georgie?" shrieked his mother as George shook violently beside her. "Are you chilly?"

"No," said George weakly, cowering away from the deathly cold fingers that were poking at his eyes. "I'm scared . . . of the dark."

"Love him!" shrilled Sharren. "Turn the lights up, Darren."

Darren lumbered over to the switch.

"So you're scared, are you, boy?" snapped Fred Feared, his bony jaw creaking on its hinge as he spoke. "Nothing we like better than seeing a bit of real fear, eh, Weird?" He thrust his bony face into George's. All George could see were two cavernous eye sockets.

"One moment, Feared," boomed his ghastly partner. "If we carry on we may scare him to death, and we were hoping to have a lot more fun with him before he dies." He waved a bony hand dismissively at the oblivious Sharren and Darren who were giggling into their cocktails. "These two are a hopeless audience. They don't appreciate a top class act. We'll have plenty of time to finish the boy off – when we have tired of experimenting on him. I haven't sawn anyone in half for a very long time."

"Indeed you are right, Weird," declared Fred Feared nastily, leaving George quivering on the sofa. "For my part I have a yearning to practise my knife throwing on the living again." He turned to his agent. "Get rid of the others, Dishwater. Little Frightley Manor is ours."

Chapter Nine

George had to make his paralysed brain think fast. If these two spiny spectres took over the haunting of Little Frightley Manor, he wouldn't last a minute once they started throwing the cutlery about. He'd end up looking worse than Mary. And what would happen to his phantom friends?

George got up slowly, edged round the glowering skeletons who were in deep discussion about his merits as a human target, and stumbled over to the far end of the lounge where Dilbert Dishwater was instructing the other competitors to leave instantly.

"Wait a minute, Mr Dishwater," he said in a whisper, so Sharren and Darren couldn't hear. "Your masters may have scared me but they haven't scared my parents."

"They are the winners of the competition," said Mr Dishwater, smirking.

"I know some ghosts who are so

73

frightening they can even scare Mum and Dad," said George in desperation.

There was silence. Everyone looked at George in amazement.

"Any ghost who can scare your parents must be truly terrifying," gasped Stanley Hollowlegs.

Mr Dishwater looked over at his masters who were now ghoulishly measuring the poker and eyeing George up. "If Mr Weird and Mr Feared cannot scare your parents, then no ghost can."

"We'll see about that!" muttered George.

Mr Dishwater began to flit anxiously backwards and forwards, trying to imagine anything more ghoulish than his two masters turning up. And trying not to imagine what Weird and Feared would do to him if it did.

Darren had joined Sharren on the sofa to watch *Gold-Diggers* on the television. George crawled on all fours round the furniture out of sight of his parents. The dreadful skeletons were busy testing the electronic grand piano to see if a body would fit in there for sawing in half. Unseen, George joined his friends behind the sofa and rapidly repeated his idea.

"A bold plan, Master George," huffed Edgar Jay shakily, "but doomed to failure, I fear. Your parents are completely lacking in spectral sensibilities."

"*And* they never see spooks," added Maggot.

"Who on earth are these awful ghosts who can scare your mum and dad?" quavered Flo.

"We don't want to be in these here waters when they arrive," growled Mary, looking for an escape route.

"Set sail!" squawked Duck.

"It's *you* lot!" whispered George. "Don't you see? You are going to have to scare my parents and win back Little Frightley Manor."

His friends gasped.

"But we can't scare anyone!"

"They'll frighten *us* off!"

"Can't scare me!" squeaked Slightly from Maggot's shirt.

A quivering list fluttered to the carpet.

A Question
by Bartholomew Otherington-Smythe

1. *I have one question for you, George.*
2. *How can we do it?*
3. *How can we possibly do it?*
4. *How do you intend us to do it?*
5. *I know that is three questions but I am terrified.*

"I'll think of something," whispered George grimly. "Stay there and come out when I whistle."

"Out yonder?" growled Mary.

"Open seas?" came Duck's muffled squawk from under the sofa.

"It's your only chance!" hissed George, ". . . and mine!"

Edgar Jay raised his nozzle importantly. It would have looked impressive if it hadn't been shaking so much.

"My dear young Ghoulstones," he huffed quietly, "we must do all we can to keep Little Frightley Manor. After all, you are the only members of your noble family left to protect your ancestral home." He caught George's eye. "Of course," he added with an embarrassed puff, "we must also save Master George from these evil skeletons."

George stood up behind the sofa. An appalling sight met his eyes. The gruesome twosome were hovering around the electronic grand piano. While George had been desperately making plans, the evil skeletons had been preparing for a performance. Laid out on the shiny lid of the piano were three knives from the kitchen, Darren's pot of cocktail sticks, and the garden axe. Being powerful and bursting with evil intent, Weird and Feared had found that, although they were ghosts, they were strong enough to carry their real and vicious props. Darren and Sharren hadn't noticed a thing. They were totally engrossed in the glittering line-up of prizes on the television screen.

"We need a volunteer from the audience," came the booming voice of Wally Weird.

A bony finger pointed at George.

"You – the boy in the back row!"

Against his will, George felt himself being drawn towards the piano. An invisible force was making him clamber over the back of the sofa towards the two waiting skeletons. Suddenly a hand with red-tipped fingers grabbed his arm. George yelped with fright.

"Stop mucking about, Georgie!" shrieked Sharren, pulling him down beside her. "You'll smudge my nail varnish. Now sit still. I can't see the telly."

But George felt himself being pulled away from his mother's grip to where Fred Feared was testing the blade of the axe.

"Won't take much of a swing, Weird," said Fred Feared nastily. "Perhaps some skewers would prolong the agony."

"Our volunteer seems to have stage fright, Feared!"

The gruesome twosome reached out with their skeletal, grasping hands and grabbed George's wrists. He felt their cold finger bones tighten round him like steel.

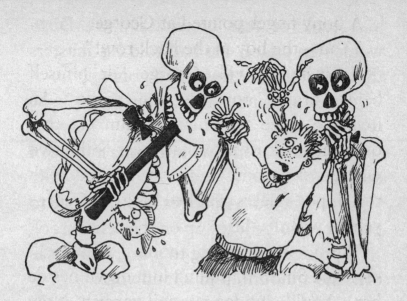

George needed help. There was only one thing for it. He gave a feeble whistle.

Slowly and with great reluctance, the seven little spooks crept round to the front of the sofa and stood there gibbering. In their astonishment at the sight, the skeletons immediately let go of George.

Mr Dishwater whooshed over and glared at the little ghosts.

"I told you all to leave!" he spat. "The competition is over."

"Dishwater!" boomed Wally Weird. "Who are these little insects?"

A look of fear crossed Dilbert Dishwater's grey face. He had told his masters that the resident ghosts had gone.

"Late entrants, Mr Weird, sir," he whimpered.

"Get rid of them! We are in the middle of our act."

Before the bony spectres had a chance to pounce, George leapt up on the piano stool.

"I present something to scare your socks off!" he announced in a loud voice.

"I don't know about scaring my socks off," shrieked his mother, "but you've certainly damaged my eardrums! Come and sit down – now!"

George sidled gratefully back to the sofa and sat between his parents. He had escaped the clutches of Weird and Feared for the moment but he was pinning his hopes of survival on a bunch of feeble phantoms who were almost invisible with fear. Why had he ever suggested that they could scare his parents?

Edgar Jay, his bag flapping with fright, raised his nozzle.

"For the honour of the Ghoulstones!" he wheezed weakly. ". . . And not forgetting Master George."

Mary nervously drew her cutlass and darted behind Flo. A piece of ghostly paper with *Whooooo!* on it trembled in the air. Duck flapped around in terrified circles. Suddenly his good eye caught sight of the two grinning skeletons and he flew straight past Darren's nose and onto his shoulder. George groaned. Even having a phantom parrot land on his shoulder wasn't going to scare Dad. Nothing scared his father except . . . George had a brainwave. He leant over and whispered in his father's ear.

Darren leapt in the air with a horrified cry, sending Duck sprawling on the coffee table.

"That's terrible! I've got to go!"

And Darren lumbered out of the room.

"What's got into him?" shrilled Sharren, not taking her eyes off the television screen.

Feeling a tiny bit more confident, Maggot waved his arms feebly at Sharren, and Edgar Jay puffed at her furry slippers.

Slightly poked his nose out of Maggot's shirt.

"Boo!" he squeaked.

This was too good an opportunity for George to miss. He murmured something to his mother.

"Ahhhhhh!" shrieked Sharren. She jumped up, gathered her housecoat around her in fear and tottered for the door, running through the gruesome twosome as she went.

Weird and Feared wobbled in the air, their bony jaws dangling open with the shock of having a shrieking Sharren run through them. The other ghosts sidled out from the corner and looked in awe at this unlikely little bunch who had proved more frightening than the two sinister skeletons.

George flung out his arm with a flourish towards his phantom friends, who had almost disappeared with fright.

"I present the Supreme Scarers of Little Frightley Manor!"

Chapter Ten

The two skeletons rattled with anger.

"*We* are top of the bill!" snapped Fred Feared, shaking his bony fist.

"Skulls and crossbones!" squawked Duck rudely.

"This feeble bunch cannot possibly be more frightening than us, Feared!" boomed Wally Weird.

"Well, they obviously are," said Stanley Hollowlegs pleasantly. Weird and Feared no longer seemed terrifying now that they had been beaten. "None of us grown-ups could make that awful living pair even blink. These little Ghoulstones are the real stars of the show."

"We share the spotlight with no one," snapped Fred Feared.

"Indeed not, Feared!" boomed Mr Weird. "Where were we before we were so rudely interrupted?"

"About to slice the boy in half, Weird!"

"Leave him be!" shouted Mary from behind Mr Hollowlegs.

"We don't want you here," called Flo, who had taken refuge in the white lady's skirts.

"We won," quavered Maggot.

"You're rubbish!" yelled Stanley Hollowlegs at the skeletons.

"Get off!" shouted the ghost in chains.

"Silence!" screeched Wally Weird in panic. "We will now perform our famed axe throwing. We will use the boy as a target."

George braced himself to resist the awful lure of the skeletons as Fred Feared grabbed hold of the axe handle. To the astonishment of the bony phantom, he found that he couldn't lift it. Now that the gruesome twosome were no longer top of the bill, their power had faded. They could do nothing to George.

"You're just a couple of bags of old bones!" he laughed. "You should both be in a joke shop!"

"We didn't come here to be insulted!" bellowed Wally Weird, rattling with fury.

"Where do you normally go then?" chuckled Stanley Hollowlegs.

Weird and Feared looked at each other. They had forgotten about hecklers after being successful for so long. They had forgotten how they'd hated the catcalls, the booing and the rotten tomatoes.

"Dishwater!" shouted Feared desperately. "Deal with these troublesome spooks."

The little Ghoulstone ghosts shimmered with fright and everyone looked around for the grey ghoul. He was nowhere to be seen. Sensing that Little Frightley Manor was going to be a rather uncomfortable place for him to stay, Dilbert Dishwater had scarpered – and in style. In the distance they could all hear the sound of the departing funeral carriage.

"We must follow him, Feared," said Wally Weird. "He is not going to get away with this!"

"Indeed, Weird!" agreed Fred Feared. "It is his fault. He must be punished. Then we will come back and finish this lot off."

They gave a deep bow, picked up their coats and swept off majestically towards the wall.

"Good riddance, you varmints!" growled Mary.

"Boo!" shouted Flo.

"I was going to say that," said Maggot.

Screwed up pieces of ghostly paper were launched from the hostile audience, knocking Wally Weird's hat off and lodging in Fred Feared's ribs. With that, the gruesome twosome sped off in haste into the garden.

Unfortunately for Wally Weird and Fred Feared, the Little Frightley phantom hunt was, at that precise moment, galloping through the front garden, in full cry. The foxhounds couldn't believe their luck when they saw the skeletons. There were enough bones for all of them.

"Well, that's a relief!" sighed the ghost in chains, finally putting his cushion down.

"Hear, hear!" said Stanley Hollowlegs. "We'll leave you Ghoulstones in peace to get on with your haunting."

"Why don't you all stay?" suggested George, who was hoping to catch another glimpse of Mr Hollowlegs' insides.

The little ghosts paled at the thought of the white lady wailing, the ghost in chains rattling and various body parts flapping about Little Frightley Manor.

"Alack!" wailed Winifred Weeping, wringing her hands. "I find I am missing my damp tower. My howls and moans just don't sound right here."

"And I've heard of a castle that needs

87

haunting," said the ghost in chains. "I won't have to do any walking. It's got a lift!" He set off on the long journey to the door.

"What about you, Mr Hollowlegs?" asked George eagerly.

"Thanks for the thought, lad," said Stanley. "But delivering that monologue has given me a taste for the stage. I fancy there'll be a vacancy now at the Hauntingdon Hippodrome."

And he and Winifred floated off together through the wall.

"We won the competition!" shouted Maggot, bouncing on a sofa.

"We can stay at Little Frightley Manor for ever!" yelled Flo.

A scrap of paper fluttered anxiously between them. *In our caravan, I hope!* it read.

"We be bold and fearless!" declared Mary, swishing her cutlass round her head.

"Phantom frighteners!" squawked Duck.

Edgar Jay trundled over to George.

"I am rather alarmed," he puffed. "It appears your parents can see us after all.

Otherwise they would not have run out of the room."

The little spooks suddenly stopped celebrating.

"No fear of that," said George, grinning as he looked at their frightened faces. "It's very simple. I was the one who scared Mum and Dad. While you were busy trying to frighten them, I told Dad that his favourite pub was being knocked down, and I whispered to Mum that there was a mouse on the carpet. I knew they'd both be off like a shot."

"So we're not scary after all," huffed Edgar Jay in relief.

"I be bold and fearless!" growled Mary, swishing her cutlass.

"Cold and fearful!" squawked Duck rudely.

Slightly suddenly woke up from a little spot of hibernation under the coffee table. He gave a fierce snuffle and tried to raise his prickles.

"What are you doing, Slightly?" asked Maggot.

"I'm protecting you all," he squeaked. "I'm a horrifying hedgehog!"

"What do you mean?" laughed Flo.

"With a ferocious snout!" squeaked the hedgehog.

"What are you going on about?" giggled George.

"*And* I can squeak boo," went on Slightly, "in a terrifying manner. You ask Mrs Brussell!"

Collect all the LITTLE TERRORS books!

The prices shown below are correct at the time of going to press. However, Macmillan Publishers reserve the right to show new retail prices on covers which may differ from those previously advertised.

JAN BURCHETT & SARA VOGLER

1. Hector the Spectre	0 330 36812 5	£2.99
2. Eerie McLeery	0 330 36813 3	£2.99
3. Bones and Groans	0 330 36815 X	£2.99
4. Knight Frights	0 330 36814 1	£2.99
5. Vampire for Hire	0 330 36816 8	£2.99
6. Ghost in the Post	0 330 36817 6	£2.99
7. Shiver and Deliver	0 330 37604 7	£2.99
8. Gruesome Twosome	0 330 37605 5	£2.99

MORE LITTLE TERRORS BOOKS FOLLOW SOON!

All Macmillan titles can be ordered at your local bookshop or are available by post from:

**Book Service by Post
PO Box 29, Douglas, Isle of Man IM99 1BQ**

Credit cards accepted. For details:
Telephone: 01624 675137
Fax: 01624 670923
E-mail: bookshop@enterprise.net

Free postage and packing in the UK.
Overseas customers: add £1 per book (paperback)
and £3 per book (hardback).